STEVEN SPIELE

A Dinosaur's Story

THE NOVELIZATION

Adapted by Cathy East Dubowski
From a screenplay by John Patrick Shanley
Based on the book by Hudson Talbott

Grosset & Dunlap • New York

ABCDEFGHIJ

Have you ever wished...

That you could see a real, live dinosaur?
That dinosaurs could come back from the past?
And that you could talk to them?
Well...How do you know they *haven't* come back?
Listen to what a little bluebird heard one sunny spring
day....

Rex Tells All

The earth was alive with the coming of spring. In a flowering tree at the edge of a golf course, a mother bluebird was feeding her nestful of chirping baby chicks.

"Hey, how about me? Where's my share?" said Buster, the smallest chick. He hadn't gotten a single worm. No matter how hard he tried to push his way into the pack, another chick always pushed him back.

Suddenly Buster found himself being pushed right out of the nest!

Unfortunately, he hadn't really learned to fly yet. He flapped his tiny, fluffy wings and tried not to look down as he plunged toward the ground.

All at once a shiny metal perch appeared out of nowhere. Buster grabbed on. Then he looked more closely at this perch. It was a golf club! And at the end of the golf club was a gigantic monster. A monster with long, sharp teeth!

"Whoa, there, little fella. Where'd you come from?"
Buster was surprised by the monster's soft, gentle voice.

"Noplace!" said Buster, trying to sound tough.

"Noplace? Never been there," said the monster. "What's your name?"

"Buster. And I'm an eagle. No—I'm a vulture. Yeah, that's what I am. A vulture." The little bluebird puffed out his chest, hoping he looked big and dangerous.

The monster grinned—and his teeth didn't look quite so scary anymore. The bluebird looked him up and down. All at once it dawned on him. "Say, ain't you a dinosaur?"

"Why, yes I am," said the dinosaur. "My name is Rex."

"Then what the heck are you doing playing golf?"

Rex smiled and took a few practice swings. "I like the fresh air," he said. Then he looked back at Buster. "Don't you have a mama somewhere who's worried about you?"

Buster looked up at his family's overcrowded nest. No one had even noticed he was gone. "Nope," he grumbled. Then his eyes gleamed. "I'm an *orphan*. My whole family was eaten by a hawk!"

"Ooh, that's terrible," said Rex—although he didn't believe a word Buster said. "So what are you going to do now?"

Buster thought a moment. He'd never been anywhere on his own before. He knew nothing about the world. "I know—I'm going to run away and join the circus!"

Rex smiled. "Ah, the circus. I knew a little fella who

2

ran away to join the circus once. You kind of remind me of him, in fact."

"I do?" said Buster.

Rex didn't answer. He was watching a butterfly dance and seemed lost in thought. "See that butterfly?" he asked Buster.

"Yeah. What about it?"

"That butterfly has a life span of only three days."

"Wow—how do you know that?"

"Because I'm smart, Buster." Rex spoke without bragging. "But I wasn't always. I started off *stupid*. And violent."

"You did?" said Buster.

"Yes," said Rex. "That was a long, long time ago, of course. I was a real terror then. I was mean. I didn't get along with my neighbors. And I was hungry all the time."

"Well, what happened?" said Buster. "What made you change?"

"It all started millions of years ago," said Rex, "when the dinosaurs walked the earth...."

2

New and Improved

Millions of years ago
Planet Earth

"Aaaarrrggghhh!" Rex's roar shook the ground.

It was the age of the dinosaurs—a time when enormous creatures roamed the earth in a constant battle for survival.

And one of the most terrifying of all was Tyrannosaurus rex.

"Aaaarrrggghhh!" Rex roared again. For miles around, dinosaurs heard him and trembled in fear.

Rex was hungry. Really hungry. And that meant trouble. Without a single supermarket on the entire planet, anything that flew, swam, walked, or ran was on the menu.

But Rex had a problem. Although he was the biggest meat-eating dinosaur, he had very small arms and hands. On top of that, he weighed nearly eight tons and couldn't run very fast. So he had a hard time catching his dinner. And that *really* made him mad.

"Aaaarrrggghhh!...Yum!" Rex spotted a tiny speckled dinosaur hiding in the tall grass. The creature turned to run—but Rex roared again, and the little dinosaur fainted.

"Heh, heh, heh." Rex laughed as he picked up the tiny creature and opened his mouth. Then the little dinosaur came to. He trembled and said his prayers as he watched Rex's sharp teeth come closer and closer....

Beep beep beep beep.

Rex looked around. What was making that unearthly sound? He didn't see anything, so he turned back to his terrified meal.

Beep beep beep beep.

Rex snarled and looked around again. This time the little dinosaur jumped free and fled into the bushes.

"Aaaarrrggghhh!" That was the third meal Rex had lost that day, and now he was madder than ever. Somebody was going to pay for this!

Beep beep beep beep.

Then Rex saw it—a glowing spaceship not much bigger than his head. It buzzed around him like a pesky mosquito. Rex slapped at it and roared.

In a moment the beeping spaceship landed, a small door opened, and a ramp shot down to the ground. A froggy-looking space creature with a propeller strapped to his back scurried out. Rex was confused.

The little space creature quickly set up a card table. He piled it high with boxes of cereal. Then he posted his signs:

BRAIN GRAIN—THE ULTIMATE VITAMIN CEREAL
FREE SAMPLES! PRIZES!

But of course Rex couldn't read.

The space creature opened his mouth as if to say something—then ran back to the spaceship and pushed a button. In seconds the ship grew ten times bigger. A sign across the ship could now be read:

BRAIN GRAIN CEREAL—THE IQ ENHANCER!
WHY BE STUPID WHEN YOU CAN EAT BRAIN GRAIN?

But of course Rex couldn't read that either.

"How do you do?" the space creature said to Rex. "My name is Vorb. And this is your lucky day! Your planet, your neighborhood—hold on to your tail now—*you* have been chosen to receive a free sample!"

Rex just stood there with his mouth hanging open.

Vorb grinned up at his very big, very surprised customer. "I have here a brand-new product. You've never seen anything like this before. Take one bite, and you'll be smart!"

Vorb picked up a few boxes. "Brain Grain comes in three flavors: nutty nut, regular, or regular very irregular. Take your pick."

Rex's eyes lit up. He took two steps toward the table. He drooled and smacked his lips as he eyed his tasty meal. But Rex wasn't looking at the cereal boxes. He was looking at Vorb.

"Can't you make up your mind?" Vorb asked, holding the boxes in front of him. "Or is it that you don't have one?"

"Aaaarrrggghhh!" Rex lunged at Vorb.

Vorb scattered his boxes and bolted for the spaceship. "That's it! I'm taking a break!"

Rex caught up with Vorb just as he ducked through the door. Rex jammed his head inside and opened his huge jaws. "Aargh!" he roared.

Quickly Vorb began dumping Brain Grain cereal down Rex's long tunnel of a throat.

Rex froze. His eyes shrank to tiny dots as light bulbs flashed over his head. His roar softened into a groan...and then a lullabylike croon.

"Aaaarrrggghhh...rrrrrrr...Row, row, row your boat, gently down the stream." Rex blinked at Vorb in surprise. "Merrily, merrily, merrily, merrily, life is but a dream."

Rex was singing—and he had a wonderful voice!

"Wh—who turned on the lights?" Rex stammered. "Hey—what am I doing? I'm *talking*!"

"Thank goodness!" said Vorb, sighing. "And it took only two hundred and eighty servings of Brain Grain to jump start that skull of yours, pal. Now then, how about some lunch?"

"Lunch? What's lunch?" Still stunned, Rex followed Vorb into the spaceship.

3

Dinosaurs Do Lunch

Deep inside the spaceship, Rex saw a strange sight. Three intelligent-looking dinosaurs were having a very friendly lunch—hot dogs, popcorn, cotton candy, and soda.

All of the dinosaurs were wearing name tags. And now Vorb slapped a tag on Rex.

"Go on—mix a little with your new friends," said Vorb. "I must report to the captain." And with that he disappeared.

Rex smiled nervously. "Hi, everybody. My name is…" He looked down and read his tag. "My name is Rex. Hey—how did I do that? I'm reading!"

A small birdlike dinosaur with wings fluttered her eyelashes at Rex. "I'm Elsa. Enchanted and delighted to meet you," she cooed.

"I'm Woog," said a chubby three-horned dinosaur. "Do you want a hot dog?"

"Are they good?" Rex asked.

"Are they good!" said Woog. "Words fail me. How many of these have we had, Dweeb?"

Dweeb was a scrawny medium-sized dinosaur with

two buckteeth. His neck pouch puffed up as he thought. "Two hundred and fifty, maybe? That's with everything on them."

"I say it's more like—*burp!*—four hundred," said Dweeb. "Believe me, Rex, you'll love them. Here, we'll make you one."

"He's *got* to try it with mustard," said Dweeb.

"Don't forget the sauerkraut!" squealed Elsa.

Rex looked on while the other dinosaurs prepared his lunch. When they shoved an overstuffed hot dog in front of him, he sniffed it. Then he took a tiny bite. Finally he smiled and gulped the rest into his mouth. "Ummm...that's what I call *lunch!*"

"Lunch—that's what you used to call *me!*" said Dweeb, and everybody laughed.

Rex looked embarrassed. "Hey, I'm sorry about the way I acted. I was a real animal."

"We've all done things we wish we hadn't," said Elsa.

"No kidding!" said Woog. "The things I've stepped on— I don't even want to think about it!"

"Up until today, you *couldn't* think about it," said Dweeb. "Let's face it—we've evolved."

The four dinosaurs looked at each other in silence. They weren't sure exactly what was going on. But they all knew that something very special had happened to them. They had changed—on the inside. And now the whole world seemed different.

"Until now, we've been uncultured," said Rex. "Now let's be friends."

It was a strange moment. Had four different kinds of dinosaurs, including a Tyrannosaurus rex, ever had lunch together—without any of them having another for the main course?

Meanwhile, the spaceship had taken off. On the ship's bridge, Vorb reported to the captain.

"How are they doing?" asked the white-haired old man as he piloted the ship.

"Terrific, Captain Neweyes," Vorb answered. "They seem happy with the results of the Brain Grain formula." He watched the captain check some readings on the control panel. "How far are we from the Middle Future, sir?"

Captain Neweyes jabbed at several blinking buttons. "Not far. I'll be down in a minute. It's time to explain things to our guests."

4

The Captain's Invention

Spaceship travelling through time

"Greetings, my friends, and welcome to my ship."

At last the four dinosaurs were meeting the captain. They were in a huge room filled with all sorts of junk— bicycles, snowshoes, nets, and a boat. Boxes overflowed with strange parts and gadgets.

The old man smiled, and his blue eyes were gentle and kind. "I am Captain Neweyes. I live in the Far Future, where all the species on the planets have learned to get along."

Even with their new, smart brains, the dinosaurs had to struggle to understand what Captain Neweyes was saying. He was from the Far Future. So what did he want with prehistoric dinosaurs?

"I've made a fortune out of my invention, Brain Grain Cereal," Captain Neweyes explained. "And now I'm trying to give something back to the universe—with this." He pointed to a small wooden object.

"This is my latest invention. It's a Wish Radio. I can

use it to hear what people are wishing for. Especially young people, because they wish the loudest."

Captain Neweyes fiddled with the knobs. Strange voices and static filled the room as he hunted for the right channel. "Ah, listen," he said at last.

I wish I had a million dollars, a boy's voice uttered.

I wish there was a singing mermaid in my swimming pool, said a girl.

I wish I had a car.

I wish my sister was nicer to me.

I wish I could fly like a bird.

"Like me!" said Elsa. "I fly."

I wish I could see a Tyrannosaurus rex!

"Captain, that's me!" said Rex. "He's talking about me!"

"That's right," said Captain Neweyes. "There are a lot of children, in this time we're listening to, who miss you. They're wishing for you. I've never heard a louder wish."

"Gosh," said Dweeb. All the dinosaurs blushed in delight.

"That's why I gave you Brain Grain," said Captain Neweyes. "Now you're smart enough to make up your own minds."

The captain pulled down a chart.

"These are the young people—the boys and girls—who want to meet you. What do you say?"

The dinosaurs looked at the children. Then they looked at each other.

"Sure!" said Woog.

"That would be swell!" said Dweeb.

"By all means!" said Elsa.

"We'll do it!" said Rex.

The excited dinosaurs all began to talk at once.

Whoop whoop whoop whoop. A sudden alarm startled them into silence.

"Captain Neweyes!" said Vorb. "We're here! We're here!"

"Thank you, Vorb," the captain said. "You may open the doors."

Then he turned to the dinosaurs and smiled. "Wait till you see this...."

5

A New World

Present day
New York City

The doors opened slowly, like the curtains at a theater. The dinosaurs stared in awe at the sights passing below.

It was just before dawn in New York City. Lights sparkled in the black night like diamonds, and skyscrapers reached toward the fading stars. The first hint of sunrise turned the edges of the sky pink.

"It's a world covered with jewels!" whispered Elsa.

"Look at all those lights!" said Rex.

"Gee whiz!" said Dweeb.

Vorb had been busy putting a parachute on the back of each dinosaur. "They're ready, Captain!"

But Captain Neweyes was not ready for them to leave just yet. "There are two people down there you should know about," he said. "One of them is there to help you." He pulled down a chart that showed a short, stout woman with glasses. "Her name is Dr. Juliet Bleeb. She knows you're coming. You'll find her at the American Museum of Natural History."

"What a nice face she has!" said Elsa.

"I'm sure you'll like her," said Captain Neweyes. Then a dark look fell across his face. "The other person you should know about is my brother—Professor Screweyes."

The captain pulled down another picture. Professor Screweyes looked a lot like Captain Neweyes. But his face held no trace of kindness. He had only one good eye—and that eye sizzled with evil.

"My brother is crazy," said Captain Neweyes. "He was driven mad by the loss of his eye many years ago. And it made him cruel. Now he travels here—in the Middle Future—causing nothing but trouble."

The dinosaurs shuddered.

"Stay clear of my brother," said Captain Neweyes. "Find Dr. Bleeb as soon as you can. Beyond that—just try not to step on anybody." The captain turned to Vorb and said, "Have you got their boat ready?"

"Aye, aye, Skipper!" Vorb answered. He shoved a big rubber raft out the door.

"Good luck!" said Captain Neweyes.

"*Bon voyage!*" said Vorb. "Take care!"

"You've got to be kidding!" cried Rex, as Vorb shoved the dinosaurs one by one out the door.

6

The Dinosaurs Take Manhattan

In these last minutes of darkness, New York City began to stir. Most New Yorkers were just waking up, brushing the sleep from their eyes. But they weren't taking the time to watch the sunrise. If they had, they would have seen an incredible sight: four dinosaurs floating by parachute into New York Harbor.

But it was impossible for one New Yorker to miss their arrival. He was a dark-haired, freckle-faced kid named Louie, who had run away from home. At that very moment he was fixing breakfast on his makeshift raft—which happened to be in the middle of New York Harbor. Right beneath the dinosaurs!

The dinosaurs' raft landed gently on the water behind Louie. He didn't even notice the ripples. But when the dinosaurs hit the water, a tidal wave flipped Louie's raft. *Smack!* Louie was tossed into the water.

The dinosaurs had no idea what they had done. Laughing and dripping, they climbed up onto their raft and freed themselves of their soggy parachutes. Dawn was spilling color across the sky and one by one the city's lights went out. How different this world was from theirs.

"Isn't it beautiful?" said Elsa with a sigh.

"What is it?" Woog wondered.

"It's Manhattan, you morons!" an angry voice shouted. "The heart of New York City!"

The dinosaurs looked down and saw Louie thrashing wildly in the water.

"Don't just sit there, help me!" he sputtered. "Help me!"

Rex fished Louie out of the harbor. Seconds later the boy stood on the dinosaur's palm, choking and coughing up water. Rex breathed on him, drying him off.

"What a bunch of jerks," Louie muttered. Then he got a good look at the huge creature who was holding him. "Hey you—what's your name?"

"Rex. What's yours?"

"Louie's the name." He looked around suspiciously at his rescuers. "What are you guys supposed to be, anyway?"

"Actually," said Elsa, "we're dinosaurs."

"Dinosaurs! Hmm, well, yeah, I guess you got that look. I mean, you're sure big enough."

"Well, you're very small," said Elsa, offended by Louie's tone of voice.

Louie put up his fists. "I'm big enough!" he cried. "I'm a grown man, understand?" He tugged at one of Elsa's wings and smirked. "What are you, a bat?"

"I'm not a bat!" exclaimed Elsa. "My name is Elsa. I'm a pterodactyl."

"So what?" said Louie, acting unimpressed. He glared at the four dinosaurs. "You know what? All my life I dreamed of building a little raft...of sailing it across New York Harbor. And joining the circus! Well, I finally got my raft. And I was on my way. Then you clowns drop out of the blue and ruin everything!"

"Gosh," said Woog. "We're sorry."

"Sorry cuts no ice with me, you goon! What I want to know is—what are you going to do about it?"

"What do you want us to do?" asked Rex.

"What do you think, you idiot?" Louie shook his head. "Help me get to the circus!"

By now the raft had drifted toward land. Louie and the dinosaurs stepped ashore.

It was growing lighter, but still the streets looked deserted. A lone street cleaner, half asleep, shuffled behind his broom.

Rex looked around, puzzled. "I thought a place with so many buildings would have more creatures in it."

Louie snickered. "What do you expect on Thanksgiving, you dope!"

"Thanksgiving? What's that?" asked Dweeb.

Louie made a face. "It's a big, dumb holiday. People are supposed to act thankful for every stupid little thing."

"What a lovely idea!" said Elsa.

"No, it's not," snapped Louie. "It's stupid. This is a tough city in a tough world. You gotta be out there with your fists up to get by."

Rex shook his head. "That's what I used to think— until I could think, that is."

"What the heck are you talking about?" said Louie.

It was funny how clear everything seemed to Rex now, as he watched Louie act tough. "It's your attitude," Rex said. "It's prehistoric. We used to be just like you—angry and always ready to fight. But we're a lot smarter now."

"Could have fooled me," Louie muttered.

Elsa and Dweeb were whispering to each other. Elsa stared at Louie a moment, then asked, "Are you a child?"

"Yeah, so? You wanna make something out of it?"

"I was just wondering where your parents are," she said.

Louie scratched his head in thought. Then his eyes gleamed. "I'm an *orphan*. My family was torn apart by a pack of wild dogs!"

Rex rolled his eyes. He and the other dinosaurs were getting a little fed up with the boy's attitude. But they had come here to meet some children. And they sensed that Louie really needed their help.

"So where's this circus you want to join, anyway?" Dweeb asked.

"Somewhere north of here, I think." Louie pulled a soggy, crumpled flyer from his pocket. He walked over to the napping street cleaner and shook him. "Yo, morning," he said. "You know where this place is?"

The street cleaner rubbed his sleepy eyes as Louie thrust the flyer under his nose. "Let me see now. The circus. That would be...somewhere in Central Park." He looked up to point the way—and saw the towering dinosaurs.

"Y-you guys d-do whatever you want! I'm gone!" The street cleaner threw down his broom and ran off.

"What's the matter with him?" called Dweeb.

"*You're* the matter, bonehead," said Louie, walking back to the dinosaurs. How the heck was he supposed to get uptown now—in the company of four dinosaurs—without starting a riot? Suddenly he had an idea.

"Hey you, batgirl! Can you fly?"

"I told you, I'm not a bat!" cried Elsa. "And yes, I can fly quite well."

"Then give me a ride," said Louie. He climbed onto her back. "I think I know a way to get to Central Park—without anybody noticing a thing."

7

Louie's Discovery

"Yee-hah!" hollered Louie as Elsa soared above Manhattan. He clung to her neck, thrilled to feel the wind in his hair. He was smiling for the first time in a long while.

"Where to?" asked Elsa.

"Go this way." Louie peered down at the ground, looking for something. "There!" he cried at last.

Far below them hundreds of people scurried about in the street. The breeze carried a faint whisper of music.

"What's that?" asked Elsa.

"That's our ticket uptown!" shouted Louie. "Hang a U-turn, Elsa. Let's go tell the others."

As she circled back, Louie saw something that nearly broke his heart. On the balcony of a tall apartment building stood a pretty girl in a fancy dress and a big hat. She was crying.

"Hit the brakes!" Louie shouted. "I've got to check this out."

Elsa landed on the railing of the balcony, and Louie jumped down. The girl screamed and backed up against the wall, trembling.

"Hey, we didn't mean to frighten you," Louie said gently. "Why are you crying?"

The girl tried to wipe away her tears. "I'm not crying!" she said.

"Come on," Louie said. "What's the matter?"

The girl shook her head, as if she didn't want to talk about it. Then she looked into Louie's blue eyes. Somehow she knew that this mysterious dark-haired boy would understand. "It's my parents."

"What's the matter—do they yell at you?"

"No," said the girl. "They're just never around. Today is Thanksgiving, and they're both off doing other things. My father's very business, and my mother's very social."

Louie nodded. "My name's Louie. What's yours?"

"Cecilia Nuthatch."

"Well, Cecilia Nuthatch, I know just how you feel. My parents have a lot of kids, and I've been getting lost in the shuffle lately. So you know what I'm doing?"

"What?" asked Cecilia.

"I'm running away to join the circus. What do you say you throw that stupid hat away and come with me?"

Cecilia looked at the freckle-faced boy. He smiled, and didn't seem tough anymore. His eyes were shining and friendly. She knew she shouldn't—couldn't—go with him. But then, who was there to care what she did?

"All right," she cried at last. "I will!" She pulled off her big, expensive hat and tossed it to the wind.

Louie grabbed her hand and pulled her over to meet Elsa.

Meanwhile, on the street below, a little girl and her mother were standing in front of a department store window. They looked longingly at a mannequin of a little girl wearing beautiful clothes and a splendid hat.

"Oh Mama, look!" said the girl. "A Thanksgiving hat!"

The mother hid a tear from her daughter. "I wish I could buy it for you, honey, but you know we're just getting by."

At that moment Cecilia Nuthatch's big, beautiful hat floated down from the sky...and landed right on the little girl's head. Mother and daughter looked toward the heavens, then at each other. "Oh, Mama!" cried the girl. They hugged one another tightly.

Then they walked down the street, so thankful for one another and for their Thanksgiving miracle that they missed another miraculous sight: a pterodactyl and two children soaring off into the clouds, ready to make their own wishes come true.

8

A Showstopping Thanksgiving

When Elsa landed, Louie introduced Cecilia to the rest of the dinosaurs. They were all impressed with her wonderful manners right away. She didn't even make a fuss about their being dinosaurs.

"Come on," Louie said. "We've got to get to Central Park. Say, where are you guys going, anyway? I mean, *after* you help us find the circus."

"We're going to the American Museum of Natural History," said Rex.

"Good," said Louie. "That's not even out of the way. I've figured out a way to get you guys through the city without starting a riot. Let's go!"

Luckily, many streets were empty because of the holiday. Louie managed to lead the dinosaurs to the busy place he and Elsa had spotted from the air.

Excited people were darting here and there. The air was filled with music from marching bands tuning their instruments. Singers were warming up their voices. Majorettes twirled their batons, then tossed them in the air. Workers hurried to put the final touches on beautifully decorated floats. Costumed crews held ropes

24

that tethered huge, colorful balloons—some as big as Rex—in the shapes of animals and cartoon characters.

"What's going on?" asked Rex.

"It's the Macy's Thanksgiving Day Parade," said Louie, proud of himself. "I figured you guys would blend right in!"

Louie and his friends soon found a place in the parade and walked along with the colorful floats and balloons. Marching bands played jolly tunes, and people along the parade route clapped and cheered. It was amazing!

Cecilia's eyes were shining as she waved to the crowds lining the street. She had never had such a wonderful time. Louie couldn't complain either. "So what do you think of my friends?" he asked her.

"I like them very much," said Cecilia, smiling. "And I like you too."

Louie's face turned red. He was happy and horrified at the same time. "Aw, cut it out," he muttered. Cecilia just kept smiling.

All of the spectators—especially the children— laughed and cheered for the dinosaurs. They thought the giant creatures were part of the parade. And the dinosaurs were having so much fun they almost forgot why they were there. Louie grinned. His plan was really going to work!

Suddenly Rex stopped in his tracks. Just ahead of him he saw something incredible. Something wonderful. Another dinosaur!

"Hey, hey, what do you know?" He made his way

up the parade line, being careful not to step on anybody. At last he reached the other dinosaur—a dinosaur just like him!

But Rex was so excited he didn't notice that the dinosaur *wasn't* just like him. He didn't notice the ropes attached to the dinosaur. And he didn't notice the marchers dressed as cavemen who held the ropes.

"Hey, nice to meet you," Rex said, smiling.

The other dinosaur didn't say a word. He stared straight ahead, bobbing up and down in the wind.

Rex wouldn't give up. "Put 'er there, pal!" he said. He grabbed the other dinosaur's hand in a hearty handshake.

Pffft! The dinosaur burst into tiny pieces that filled the air like confetti.

Elsa screamed. The people watching the parade began screaming too. The band stopped playing. The majorettes collided with the band members. The float next to the dinosaurs slammed on its brakes, and sent the folk dancers tumbling into a pile.

Louie stared openmouthed at the confusion surrounding his new friend Rex. Before he could think of what to do, sirens drowned out the yelling from the crowd. In seconds, police cars swarmed the area.

Rex stood there, gazing in surprise at a piece of rubber in his hand. The other dinosaur had not been a real dinosaur at all—just a giant parade balloon!

"Quick!" Louie shouted to Rex and the other dinosaurs. "Split up—and run! We'll meet you in Central Park!"

9

The Path in the Park

Rex stood in the middle of the street, looking confused. "Central Park?" he asked. "Where is that?" But he didn't have much time to wonder, because right then he noticed a poster stuck on a wall:

PROFESSOR SCREWEYES' ECCENTRIC CIRCUS,
NOW APPEARING IN CENTRAL PARK.

Rex stared at the poster. "Professor Screweyes is that evil guy the captain warned us about," he said to himself. Then everything sank in.

"Hey," he yelled to his friends. "Louie and Cecilia are in trouble! We've got to help them!" But Rex's friends had already scattered in every direction—running from the police. Rex took off too—as fast as he could.

After a long chase through the streets, Rex discovered a hiding place in an abandoned building. And there he found his friends, already hiding.

"Rex!" Woog greeted him. "We were worried about you."

"The police were everywhere!" Rex said, huffing. "But I managed to get away."

"That sure was close," added Dweeb.

"Well, we're all together now," Elsa said. "That's what's important."

At that instant there was a huge explosion, and the dinosaurs went soaring through the air. With four loud thuds, they landed in Central Park.

A bright yellow taxi screeched to a halt at the curb near an entrance to the park. Louie and Cecilia paid the driver and got out. Quickly the taxi drove off, leaving the two children alone.

Strange...most of the park was filled with happy, excited people. But not this part. It seemed empty. Still, somewhere out there was the Eccentric Circus. And Louie was determined to find it.

Ahead of them he and Cecilia saw a path overshadowed by dark, twisted trees. Louie looked at the map on his flyer. "This must be right. The map says this path is the way to the circus. Come on."

Cecilia held Louie's hand as they ran down the dark path. The sudden squawk of a crow made the two kids jump.

"It's hard to see in here, huh?" said Louie.

Cecilia looked nervously at the crooked trees on both sides of the winding path. The branches tangled overhead in an eerie canopy. "It's a little creepy, don't you

think?" she whispered. "Are you sure this is the right way?"

"Hey, Cecilia, look!" Louie had spotted another flyer, and he ran ahead to read it. It said:

PROFESSOR SCREWEYES' ECCENTRIC CIRCUS
RIGHT THIS WAY

The two children kept going. The farther they walked, the quieter it grew. The trees and bushes were thicker now. And so far they hadn't seen another living soul.

Cecilia looked over her shoulder and clutched at Louie's sleeve. "Maybe we should turn back."

"No way," he said. "By now, we must be close. Look— another sign."

This flyer was taped to the side of an old garbage can. It said:

PROFESSOR SCREWEYES' ECCENTRIC CIRCUS
Maybe you should stop right here.

Stop right here? It was a little eerie.

Louie and Cecilia looked at each other. What should they do?

10

No Turning Back

Suddenly a screeching black cat leaped out of the garbage can. Louie and Cecilia screamed and ran—deeper into the trees. The path became harder to follow. Cecilia pulled Louie to a stop.

"I hate to say this, Louie—but it's getting awfully dark. I think we should turn back."

"Well..." Louie looked around. Maybe she was right. But he hated to give up. Especially when they were so close. He looked back over his shoulder, then peered farther down on the path. "Wait a minute! There it is!"

Cecilia followed him as he ran. Up from the gloom rose a giant black tent. A dim golden light glowed from within.

Every now and then a small group of people scurried out like frightened mice. Some looked worried. Others looked angry. But they all looked frightened.

"Come on," whispered Louie. "Let's go see what's inside."

The two crept up to the entrance. A woman in a dark coat nearly knocked them down as she rushed out, clutching her purse. She glared at them, her eyes filled with anger and fear. Then without a word she hurried off.

Cecilia and Louie looked at each other...then peeked in.

At first it was so dark they could hardly see a thing. They inched their way inside, and after a while they could make out shapes. In the center of a dim spotlight stood a tall man. The smoke from his long black cigarette hung around his head like a polluted cloud.

"That must be Professor Screweyes," Louie whispered.

A short, fat clown with curly hair and a big red nose tumbled in front of him. Each time the tall man snapped his fingers, the clown did a new trick. But no matter what the poor little clown did, the tall man didn't respond: he didn't laugh or smile or even frown. He just took another puff from his cigarette.

The clown didn't seem to mind, though. He performed his tricks cheerfully and only smiled when he got no reaction. Cecilia thought he was charming, and she laughed out loud.

Professor Screweyes looked around. "Who laughed?" he demanded.

Louie spoke before Cecilia could. "I did!"

"No, it was me, sir." Cecilia insisted.

Professor Screweyes glared at the clown. "Stubbs, get out of here." With a nod, the little clown waddled off into the shadows.

"Sorry, kids, you missed the show." Professor Screweyes' voice was deep and threatening.

Louie stepped closer, unafraid. "But we're not here to see the show. We ran away from home—we want to join up."

"Well, you ran away to the wrong circus, kid."

"What do you mean?" said Louie. "You don't want us?"

"Come on, Louie." Cecilia tugged at his arm. "I think we should go."

Professor Screweyes puffed on his cigarette and studied the children carefully for a moment. Then he sneered. "I'll take you if you want."

"Louie, please!" cried Cecilia. "I'm not so sure we—"

"Standard contract," the professor added. He pulled a formal-looking piece of paper from his coat pocket. At the bottom were a black ribbon and a red wax seal. Other than that the contract was blank.

"But there's nothing written on this contract," said Louie.

"I try to keep things simple," the professor responded. Without warning he pricked Louie's finger.

"Ouch!" Louie watched a single drop of blood bead up on his fingertip.

"Press it to the contract," Professor Screweyes commanded in a hypnotic voice. Louie's finger slowly neared the paper.

"No, Louie!" cried Cecilia. "I'm scared!"

"You are?" Professor Screweyes smiled. "Good!" He

grabbed Louie's wrist and roughly pressed the boy's finger to the contract.

At once the paper filled with words, in languages Louie couldn't understand. He gasped. His bloodstain on the bottom of the crisp white paper curled into a signature: *Louie*.

When Cecilia saw what had happened, she pricked her own finger and then pressed it to the paper below Louie's name. Shuddering, she watched the bloodstain twist into the letters of her name: *Cecilia*. Then she took a deep breath and stared boldly into Professor Screweyes' single, mocking eye.

"Well, kids," the professor said smoothly. "Welcome to Professor Screweyes' Eccentric Circus."

Louie and Cecilia grabbed one another's hand. Their dream of joining the circus had come true... only it was beginning to feel more like a nightmare.

❚❚ Dinosaurs to the Rescue

"Yoo-hoo! Louie! Cecilia! Where are you?"

Professor Screweyes whirled around, startled. "Who's that?"

"Louie! Where are you, pal?"

"It's okay," said Louie. "It's some friends of mine."

The two children headed toward the tent opening. But suddenly Professor Screweyes was standing between them, holding each by an arm.

It was night now, and the lights of the city glittered in the distance. But even a full moon could not chase away the pitch-black gloom that surrounded Professor Screweyes' tent.

The professor stared at four large shapes moving about in the darkness. When they stepped into the dull light that spilled from the tent, the professor cried out in surprise.

Four living, breathing dinosaurs! He was frightened—but also fascinated.

"Louie! Cecilia!" cried Dweeb. "Get away from that man!"

"Hey, chill," said Louie. "We just joined his circus!"

"But Louie," Rex cried. "That's Professor Screweyes! We were warned about him!"

Professor Screweyes scowled and stepped in front of the children. "Warned? By whom?"

"Your brother," said Rex.

"So that's how you got here...and why you can talk," said the professor. "He's fed you that Brain Grain stuff, hasn't he? And he warned you about me, did he?" He spat on the ground. "Let him mind his own business!"

The professor then stopped and tried to calm himself down. "Did he show you that silly Wish Radio of his?"

"Yeah!" said Dweeb. "We heard what people wish for."

Professor Screweyes smiled. "I have a radio too. Let me show it to you."

"No way," said Rex. He reached out to take Louie and Cecilia. "We don't want anything to do with you. Come on, kids, we'll take you to the Museum of Natural History with us."

"Stop!" Professor Screweyes whipped out the children's contract and waved it at Rex. "They're not going anywhere. They're under contract to me—for a very, very long time."

The dinosaurs looked at each other helplessly. Cecilia began to cry. Louie put his arm around her. "Hey, come on," he said. "It's going to be all right."

"I don't think so," said Professor Screweyes. His eye glowed with the spark of an idea. "Unless...we can work something out with your friends here." With a smug smile he turned and took the children back into his tent.

He knew the dinosaurs would follow.

12

The Professor's Invention

Inside the tent Professor Screweyes brought out a small, plain radio. He waited for everyone to gather round. Then he spoke in a low, spooky voice, as if telling a ghost story.

"This is the time of strong wishes, yes," he said. "But even stronger fears. This is my Fright Radio. It picks up what scares people most." The professor turned the radio on. At first it emitted only static.

"I find out what people are afraid of. Then I give it to them. Consider it a public service. The people who come to my circus come to get scared out of their wits." He chuckled wickedly. "And I make sure they get what they want."

"Good grief!" Louie whispered to Cecilia. "That's why all those people were running out of the tent looking so scared."

Professor Screweyes turned the radio dial—and all at once a huge, ugly spider ran up to Rex, who screamed.

The professor laughed. He turned the knob again, and a cobra snaked its head into the air. Another twist, and a ball of fire streaked across the room. Each time the children and the dinosaurs cried out, more and more afraid.

"But this is the station that comes in loudest of all." The professor twiddled the knob until voices came in clearly.

There's something in the closet, I know it! someone moaned.

Hello? Who's there? Answer me! another voice cried.

I saw a movie about a monster last night. It gave me nightmares.

A monster's going to eat me if I go in there!

There's a monster under my bed!

"Do you see what they're most afraid of, my friends?" The professor looked around. When no one spoke, he answered: "Monsters."

Rex gulped and looked around nervously. "Monsters?"

"*You!*" said the professor, his mind at work. "With a little help, that is." He reached into his coat pocket and pulled out a bottle of glowing green pills. On the label was a skull and crossbones.

"What's that?" asked Cecilia.

"Brain Drain," said Professor Screweyes. "It's the antidote to my brother's goody-goody Brain Grain Cereal." He eyed his prehistoric visitors. Their kind, intelligent faces made him sick. "These pills will take you back. Back to the way you were before. They'll make you monsters again!"

"Forget it," said Rex. "We'll just say no."

38

"Fine," said Professor Screweyes. "You're free to go. But the children," he added, "are mine."

The professor pulled out the contract again. His good eye began to spin, like a green and black pinwheel. Louie and Cecilia tried not to look, but they couldn't help it. Professor Screweyes was hypnotizing them.

Soon the two children stood in a trance, their mouths hanging open. Professor Screweyes took one of the glowing green pills from the bottle. He cracked it in two and popped one of the halves into each child's mouth.

"This is only a tiny, temporary dose," he said. "Just to give you a hint of what these little pills can do."

In seconds Louie and Cecilia began to change. Their eyes dimmed. Their words came out as monkey chatter, and they scampered around the circus ring like frantic animals.

"Oh, what's he done to them!" cried Elsa.

"Change them back," Rex said angrily, "or I'll—"

"Or you'll what?" asked Professor Screweyes. He laughed in Rex's face. "You won't hurt me, you weakling. My brother's Brain Grain has changed you. You've lost your prehistoric savagery. You're no longer powerful and violent—you're *civilized* now. So you'll respect this contract just like the chump you are."

Rex felt trapped, helpless. If this problem had come up in the past, he would have solved it with one big bite. Now he knew that was wrong. But how could he save his friends?

Professor Screweyes watched the confusion in Rex's eyes with glee. "However, I might be willing to bargain with you."

"Anything," said Rex.

The professor smiled. "Simple. You all agree to take this Brain Drain—and I'll tear up the children's contract. If you don't take the Brain Drain, I'll put them in my circus and use them to scare people. It's up to you."

Rex looked over at Louie and Cecilia. Exhausted, they had fallen asleep on the ground. The pill must be wearing off, Rex thought, because they were beginning to look like themselves again. One glance at their innocent, sleeping faces, and Rex's mind was made up.

"I'll take it," said Rex.

"Us too," said Elsa, Dweeb, and Woog.

"Wonderful!" exclaimed Professor Screweyes. "Come with me. You're all going to be *wild* again!" He laughed like a delighted child as the dinosaurs followed him obediently. Meanwhile, the sleeping children dreamed of circus clowns and monsters.

13

A Dose of Evil

Rex stared out through the strong iron bars of his cage. He was surrounded by hundreds of black crows, whose eerie *caws* filled the air.

Nearby, Elsa, Woog, and Dweeb were locked in their own cages.

"What I wouldn't give for a hot dog," said Woog.

"Oh, yes—with sauerkraut," said Elsa.

"And remember those yummy buns?" said Dweeb with a sigh.

They stared in front of them at what they would be eating instead: a huge barrel full of Brain Drain pills.

Professor Screweyes hurried into the tent carrying a large box with a label that read "Pill Gun." He pulled out a big, strange-looking gun and began pouring pills into it.

The professor grew chatty as he filled the pill gun. "My brother probably didn't tell you, but I lost my eye because of a crow. I was a boy when it happened."

"How awful!" said Elsa.

"Yes," Professor Screweyes said angrily. Then he

looked up at the crows that filled the tent. "I'm afraid of crows now, so I keep them with me. Do you find that odd? It's simple, really. I am afraid of them, but I am also their master. I am the master of my fear!"

"This guy is nuts!" Rex said to the others.

"Now then," said the professor, holding up the pill gun. "Who'd like to go first?"

"Wait," said Rex. "You have to destroy the children's contract."

"Oh, all right." The professor pulled out the contract and set it on fire. He sniffed the black smoke as if it were perfume. Then he picked up the pill gun once more. "Now," he said, stopping in front of Rex's cage, "open wide."

The dinosaurs shook with fear, and their cages rattled.

"Are you afraid?" asked Professor Screweyes. "That's good—*very* good!" He laughed madly and fired a blast of pills into Rex's mouth. Rex swallowed....

And he began to change. His eyes glazed over. His face twisted into a beastly snarl. His hands clawed angrily at the bars of his prison.

"Aaaarrrggghhh!"

Elsa, Dweeb, and Woog remembered the blood-curdling roar of Tyrannosaurus rex and trembled. Only now the scream was even more terrifying. For Rex not only was a beast again—he sounded as if he had gone insane!

And they knew they were next.

"Yes!" Professor Screweyes cried in delight. "Give in to that prehistoric rage! Senseless, bloodthirsty creatures, that's what you'll be. You'll terrify my miserable audience!"

The professor smiled as he reloaded his gun. "Oh, how you will satisfy their fears."

14

Bad News from a Clown

The long night ended, and the sun rose over Central Park. Bluebirds chased away the shadows of the night with their song. But in one corner of the park, midnight's darkest fears had become real.

Cecilia was awakened by sunlight on her face. She rubbed her eyes, unsure of where she was at first. Then she saw Louie, still snoring away. Smiling tenderly, she brushed the hair out of his eyes. She tickled him under his nose, and he woke up sneezing.

"Good morning," she said, laughing.

"Morning," said Louie, rubbing his nose.

"Good morning," they heard someone else say. They turned and saw Stubbs, the little clown, holding a breakfast tray.

"Oh, look," Cecilia said. "It's that funny clown."

"I brought you breakfast," Stubbs said. "Pancakes okay?"

"Oh yes, thank you," said Cecilia.

Stubbs served the pancakes, and the hungry children dug into their food.

"So," the clown asked shyly, "you thought I was funny, huh?"

"Oh yes, very funny," Cecilia said.

"Mmm-mmm," said Louie with a mouthful of pancakes.

For the first time the children saw Stubbs frown. "The professor never laughs at what I do."

"You don't get it, do you?" said Louie. "That guy's crazy."

"Look," said the clown, "he told me you've got to get out of here right after breakfast."

"What about our contract?" asked Louie.

"He burned it," said Stubbs.

Louie and Cecilia looked at one another in surprise.

"That's lucky," said Cecilia.

But Louie was troubled. "What about our friends?"

"Forget them," said Stubbs. "And just get out of here."

Louie shoved his plate out of the way. He didn't like the sound of this. "Where are they, Stubbs? Come on, tell me!"

The clown sighed. "All right. I'll tell you. But you're not going to like it."

Cecilia and Louie were horrified when they heard what had happened to the dinosaurs. Professor Screweyes would never let the children near them now. How were they going to help their friends?

"Well," said Stubbs, "I have an idea." He looked around nervously and lowered his voice. "A way for you to get close to the dinosaurs."

Louie and Cecilia leaned closer.

"But you'll have to wait until tonight's show...."

15

Professor Screweyes' Eccentric Circus .

The big black tent was packed that night for Professor Screweyes' Eccentric Circus. Three goblins stood at the entrance, scaring people as they arrived.

"Oooooo-eeeeeeee!" shrieked one of the goblins.

"*Boooooo!* You buncha dopes!" yelled the second.

The third one let out a tiny "Boo..."

"Is that the best you can do?" Louie whispered from under his goblin costume.

"I don't want to scare people," said Cecilia.

"Well, neither do I," Louie said. "But if we don't do a good job, we'll get caught."

"Oh, all right." Cecilia sighed and made a face at a man going by. He screamed and ran inside. "I don't understand these people," she said.

"Don't you see?" said Stubbs. "That's why they come. To get scared. Simple as that."

A small band began to play spooky music. People jostled one another to get good seats. Stubbs, Louie, and Cecilia hurried off to join the opening act. They had to find a way to set the dinosaurs free. And soon!

Professor Screweyes appeared in the spotlight in the

center ring. "Ladies and gentlemen! Welcome to the most terrifying show on planet Earth—Professor Screweyes' Eccentric Circus! We will scare you. We will terrify you. We will shock you witless with our terrible, horrifying, monstrous program! And now, without further ado, I give you the Grand Demon Parade!"

Stubbs, Louie, and Cecilia were backstage on a float of demons, pulled by a team of black horses. "This is it," Stubbs whispered. "Just wave your pitchforks and look scary!"

The parade pulled out into the center ring. There were jackals and hyenas and elephants in chains. Demons and goblins danced around cackling witches. Cavemen shook spiked clubs. People in the audience screamed and opened their mouths wide. But not a soul got up to leave.

"What's wrong with these people?" Cecilia whispered.

"I don't know," Louie whispered back. "But I've never seen so many tonsils in all my life."

The band began to play hypnotic jungle music. Sixteen elephants entered the ring, pulling a huge platform from which rose a pyramid as big as an apartment building. Cavemen with burning torches circled the pyramid as it stopped in the center of the ring.

"Ladies and gentlemen," Professor Screweyes shouted, "I give you the most fearsome creatures of your darkest dreams. I give you... *monsters!*"

The cavemen tugged at some ropes, and the sides of the pyramid fell away. The audience shrieked in terror.

16

The Beasts Unleashed

Four giant monsters—prehistoric dinosaurs—stood on the platform, struggling wildly against their chains.

The audience was in an uproar.

"This is horrible!" Cecilia cried. "What can we do?"

"I don't know," Louie said helplessly. "Think!"

Professor Screweyes was thrilled at the confusion. "Ladies and gentlemen!" he shouted. "I will now attempt the impossible. I will attempt to master the most fearsome of all the dinosaurs—the mighty Tyrannosaurus rex!"

The spectators calmed down a little as they watched in fascinated horror.

The professor stared at Rex, and his eye began to spin once more into a green and black pinwheel. "Look into my eye, you bloodthirsty monster!"

Rex let out a deafening roar and swung a mighty claw at Professor Screweyes. Then his eyes turned glassy. He was hypnotized!

The professor was pleased. "Remove the chains!" he ordered the cavemen. The audience gasped as the cavemen obeyed. Rex didn't move.

"Take two steps," the professor ordered.

Rex took two steps.

"Now take two steps toward the audience."

Rex took two steps toward the audience. The people screamed.

Professor Screweyes was tickled pink. "You're terrified of this monster!" he cried to the audience. "But he does what I say. I am the Master of Fear! I am not afraid!"

As Professor Screweyes rambled on, one of the big, black crows began to peck away at a control box that read "Don't Touch." All of a sudden, fireworks went off throughout the tent.

Rex froze. He blinked. The fireworks had awakened him from his trance. He roared angrily and turned toward Professor Screweyes. Terrified, the professor tried to run away. But Rex snatched him up in his claws. The audience shouted louder than ever. The professor's screams were the loudest of all.

"He's gonna eat Professor Screweyes!" cried Stubbs.

Louie couldn't stand it any longer. He ran to his friend Rex. Cecilia tried to stop him, but Stubbs held her back.

Rex was drooling as he squeezed Professor Screweyes tightly. He was just about to eat him.

"No!" Louie shouted. "Don't do it!"

Rex looked down at the small boy for a moment, confused. Then he turned back to the professor and opened his mouth wide.

Louie wouldn't give up. "Rex, don't do it, I'm telling

you! I know you can't understand me, but you gotta!"

Cecilia watched, terrified. She closed her eyes tightly for a minute and wished with all her might. "Oh, please, please, let no more bad happen!"

"Rex!" Louie cried. "You don't want to be like them. Don't ruin everything just because you're mad or scared or something! It can't be all about that, or what's life for?"

The audience was spellbound as it watched this small boy face the raging monster.

"I know I act like I'm the original tough guy," Louie went on. "But that's 'cause I'm scared too. But you, Rex, you've got nothing to prove. You're a giant. Rex—that means 'king.' Be a king, Rex. Don't be just another slob ruining the way the world could be. Be better than everybody else. Put him down, Rex. Please!"

Rex grew quiet and stared down at the boy. His brain was still that of a prehistoric animal. But somewhere deep inside stirred a memory. A memory of a different world.

Rex opened his hand. Professor Screweyes fell to the ground.

As the audience cheered, Louie reached up to hug his friend. "Way to go, Rex!" Though still a beast, Rex smiled.

Instantly the top of the tent was torn away. A glowing spaceship hovered in the night sky. A laser shot down from the ship and zapped the chains, setting the dinosaurs free.

Cecilia couldn't believe it—her wish was coming true!

A mechanical arm came down from the spaceship and aimed funnels into the dinosaurs' mouths. Another arm snaked down and dumped Brain Grain Cereal into the funnels.

In seconds the dinosaur roars turned into rounds: "Row, row, row your boat, gently down the stream..." Rex, Elsa, Woog, and Dweeb were back! Their eyes shone with intelligence once more. They hugged one another. They were all right!

The spaceship landed. Then the door opened, and down came a ramp. Captain Neweyes climbed out and walked over to where Professor Screweyes lay in the dirt.

"Hello, brother," he said.

"I should have known you were behind this!" croaked the professor.

Captain Neweyes shook his head. "It wasn't me. You'd already lost by the time I arrived. This boy had beaten you."

The captain walked over to Cecilia and shook her hand. "I heard your wish on my Wish Radio. 'Let no more bad happen.' Very good. I couldn't agree more."

Cecilia smiled at the captain, then ran to Louie. "You were great!" she said, and gave him a great big kiss. Rex laughed as Louie turned red for the second time.

"Okay, everybody on board," Captain Neweyes called out.

"What about me?" cried Professor Screweyes. He was

still lying in the dirt where Rex had dropped him.

Captain Neweyes eyed his brother with a mixture of pity and disgust.

Stubbs came over too and looked down at his boss. "I thought I could make you laugh. That's why I stayed. Stupid me. Well, these folks think I'm funny. So I'm quitting. I'm going to find a good circus, one where the people come to be happy." Whistling joyfully, he waved good-bye to his new friends and walked away.

"Where do you think you're going!" Professor Screweyes yelled. "Come back here!"

But Stubbs kept whistling and disappeared into the night.

"We're going now too," said Captain Neweyes.

"But brother!" cried the professor. "When I'm alone, when I have no one to scare, I get very scared myself." He pointed at the black-feathered shadows. "The crows!"

"Will you change your ways and come with me?" asked the captain.

"Never!"

"Then we must leave you." Captain Neweyes led his friends into the spaceship. Seconds later they took off, leaving Professor Screweyes alone with his fears.

17

A Special Friend

New York was covered in the early darkness of a November evening. No one seemed to notice as four huge dinosaurs, two children, an old man, and a small space creature climbed the steps of the American Museum of Natural History.

"I can't believe we're finally here!" Elsa said.

"What a neat building!" said Dweeb.

Rex tried to go inside, but the door was locked.

"Hmm," said Captain Neweyes, looking at his watch, "the museum must be closed."

Rex pounded on the door, and the sound could be heard echoing through the museum. Soon quick footsteps tapped along the halls, approaching the door. And then it opened.

In the dim light stood a short, plump woman. She peered up through her glasses at the dinosaurs and gasped. But instead of screaming, she burst into delighted laughter.

"Come in, come in!" she exclaimed, flinging the door open wide. "I've been waiting for you!"

Just as Captain Neweyes had promised, Dr. Juliet Bleeb was a wonderful person. "Welcome! Welcome!" she said, ushering everybody inside.

"I've arranged a little surprise for you," Dr. Bleeb continued. She led her guests down a long hall. Then she grinned and opened a set of big doors.

"Oh, boy!" said Rex.

Inside were several long tables set for a party. There were flowers everywhere. And the tables were covered with popcorn, cotton candy, soda, and plenty of mustard and sauerkraut—for the dinosaurs' favorite food.

"Hot dogs!" cried Woog. The dinosaurs stampeded into the room, with Louie and Cecilia right behind them. Dr. Bleeb watched the happy creatures with pleasure.

"This is awfully nice of you," said Captain Neweyes.

"Nonsense," said Dr. Bleeb, blushing. "Once in a lifetime. A dream come true, don't you know. I've been wishing for this since I was a little girl."

Everybody had a wonderful time at the party. Then cushions and blankets were spread out on the floor so the dinosaurs and the children could sleep.

Dr. Bleeb tucked the guests in for the night. When she spoke, her voice was as soothing as that of a mother telling a bedtime story.

"I'm sure you'll sleep well," she said, arranging pillows under Rex's head. "Tonight you will have sweet dreams. And tomorrow you'll begin to fulfill the wishes of many children."

"How will we do that?" Rex asked sleepily.

"You'll see," said Dr. Bleeb. "It will be our secret. And it will be very good. Very good, indeed."

She turned the lights off then, and she and Captain Neweyes tiptoed to the door.

The dinosaurs and the children cuddled up together, and were soon asleep.

18
What the Children Saw

It was a bright, crisp day in early December. The weather in New York City was brisk and cold, but still the lines were long at the American Museum of Natural History. A banner draped across the front of the building announced a new dinosaur exhibit:

WE'RE BACK!

Inside the museum Dr. Bleeb was leading a group to the dinosaur exhibit hall. She stopped at the door and turned. "Thank you," she told the grown-ups, shooing them away. "I will take the children from here, please."

Once inside the exhibit hall with the children, Dr. Bleeb carefully closed the door. The children looked at the dinosaurs. The huge creatures were so still they looked like statues.

Dr. Bleeb made sure she and the children were alone in the hall—that no grown-ups besides her could hear or see. Then she giggled. "Okay—go for it!"

And the dinosaurs came to life—to the delighted squeals of the children.

56

A boy ran over to Rex and smiled. "Hi, I'm Max."

"Hi, Max. I'm Rex." The gigantic dinosaur winked at the boy. "This will be our little secret, okay?"

19

Sweet Dreams

Present day
A golf course, somewhere in the United States

"And that's exactly what happened, Buster," Rex was saying to his new little bluebird friend. "The other dinosaurs and I still live at the museum. Louie and Cecilia went home and made up with their parents. Those kids are quite a couple now. And once in a while, I sneak out to play a little golf."

Rex looked fondly at Buster, who had fallen asleep on his nose.

Gently he lifted the bluebird up to his nest and tucked him in among all his brothers and sisters. "Good night, little tough guy. Remember my story."

Rex looked up at the sky as darkness fell and the first stars began to twinkle. He smiled as he watched a spaceship soar over the golf course and zoom on toward New York City.

The lights of the skyscrapers began to sparkle against the darkening sky. For a moment the glowing spacecraft added one more light to the glittering array. Then it disappeared into the Far Future.

All over the city, children closed their eyes and thought about the secret at the American Museum of Natural History. The dinosaurs were back! And a wonderful wish had come true.

THE END